Manushkin, Fran,
The mystery of the fishy
canoe /
[2023]
33305254217700
ca   03/14/23

WOO and PEDRO Mysteries

The Mystery of the Fishy Canoe

by Fran Manushkin

illustrated by Tammie Lyon

PICTURE WINDOW BOOKS
a capstone imprint

Published by Picture Window Books, an imprint of Capstone
1710 Roe Crest Drive, North Mankato, Minnesota 56003
capstonepub.com

Text copyright © 2023 by Fran Manushkin
Illustrations copyright © 2023 by Capstone

All rights reserved. No part of this publication may be reproduced in whole or in part, or stored in a retrieval system, or transmitted in any form or by any means, electronic, mechanical, photocopying, recording, or otherwise, without written permission of the publisher.

Library of Congress Cataloging-in-Publication Data is available on the Library of Congress website.

ISBN: 9781484673973 (hardcover)
ISBN: 9781484673935 (paperback)
ISBN: 9781484673942 (ebook PDF)

Summary: Katie and Pedro are headed out for an afternoon of canoeing with their moms. But Katie and her mom get separated from the other canoe, and before long, Pedro and his mom grow worried. Where could their friends have gone? The search is on for Katie Woo and her fishy canoe.

Design Elements by Shutterstock: Darcraft, Magnia
Designed by Dina Her

Printed and bound in the USA. PO5195

Table of Contents

Chapter 1

A Canoe Ride

It was a warm, sunny day.

"Surprise!" said Pedro's
mom. "We are going on a
canoe ride."

"Cool!" said Pedro.

"Guess what?" said

Pedro's mom. "Katie and

her mom are coming too."

"Terrific!" yelled Pedro.

"That makes it more fun."

Pedro and his mom got

into a canoe.

"Oops!" said Katie's mom.

"I forgot my hat in the car.

You go ahead, and Katie

and I will catch up."

"There's a lot to see here,"

said Pedro's mom.

"Great!" said Pedro. "I don't

want to miss anything. I hope

Katie sees everything too."

"Look!" yelled Pedro. "I see a Great Blue Heron's nest."

"Awesome!" said his mom.

"The babies are not very cute," said Pedro.

"They'll be cute someday," said Pedro's mom.

Pedro looked around. "Katie and her mom should be here by now. I wonder where they are?"

"I'm sure they are fine,"
said Pedro's mom. "They are
probably just taking their
time and paddling slowly."

Chapter 2

Trouble Brewing

Pedro and his mom

passed pretty pink water

lilies.

"These flowers smell

sweet!" Pedro smiled. "But I

can't stop thinking of Katie."

"Watch out!" warned Pedro's
mom. "You are rowing us in
circles."

"Sorry!" said Pedro.

Pedro and his mom rowed

harder. Before long, their

canoe was going straight

again. But soon there was

more trouble!

Suddenly, clouds covered the sun, and the wind blew harder.

"Oh no!" said Pedro. "It's starting to rain. Now I'm extra worried about Katie."

"Maybe the wind turned

Katie's canoe upside down!"

said Pedro. "Maybe she

needs our help!"

"Let's go back the way we came," said Pedro's mom. "We will find Katie and her mom and help them."

"Which way was that?" asked Pedro.

"I don't know!" said his mom.

Chapter 3

The Search

"I know what to do,"

said Pedro. "Let's follow that

smell. It's coming from the

water lilies we passed. Katie

and her mom must have

passed them too."

They paddled their canoe to

the water lilies.

No Katie! No Mom!

"Oh my!" said Pedro's mom.

"I have another idea," said

Pedro.

"Let's go back to another thing we passed: the Great Blue Heron's nest! Maybe Katie and her mom went back there."

Pedro and his mom paddled

to the nest.

No Katie! No Mom!

"Let's hurry back to shore,"

said Pedro's mom. "We must

tell the police Katie and her

mom are lost."

Pedro and his mom

paddled fast, fast, fast.

"Stop!" yelled Pedro.

"I see Katie's canoe."

It was empty!

"Oh no!" Pedro groaned.

"I hope they didn't drown!"

"No way!" said Pedro's

mom. "Look at the shore.

They are sitting on a log,

holding fishing poles!"

"Yay!" yelled Pedro.

"What a great sight!"

Katie told Pedro, "Mom and I wanted to surprise you with fish for supper."

"You sure did," said Pedro. The fish was very tasty!

About the Author

Fran Manushkin is the author of Katie Woo, the highly acclaimed fan-favorite early-reader series, as well as the popular Pedro series. Her other books include *Happy in Our Skin*, *Plenty of Hugs!*, *Baby, Come Out!*, and the best-selling board books *Big Girl Panties* and *Big Boy Underpants*. There is a real Katie Woo: Fran's great-niece, but she doesn't get into as much trouble as the Katie in the books. Fran lives in New York City, three blocks from Central Park, where she can often be found bird-watching and daydreaming. She writes at her dining room table, without the help of her naughty cats, Goldy and Chaim.

About the Illustrator

Tammie Lyon, the illustrator of the Katie Woo and Pedro series, says that these characters are two of her favorites. Tammie has illustrated work for Disney, Scholastic, Simon and Schuster, Penguin, HarperCollins, and Amazon Publishing, to name a few. She is also an author/illustrator of her own stories. Her first picture book, *Olive and Snowflake*, was released to starred reviews from *Kirkus* and *School Library Journal*. Tammie lives in Cincinnati, Ohio, with her husband, Lee, and two dogs, Amos and Artie. She spends her days working in her home studio in the woods, surrounded by wildlife and, of course, two mostly-always-sleeping dogs.

Glossary

awesome (AW-suhm)—extremely good

canoe (kuh-NOO)—a small, shallow boat that people move through water with paddles

Great Blue Heron (GRAYT BLOO HAIR-uhn)—a gray-blue bird with a long bill, long legs, and a long neck

tasty (TAY-stee)—good tasting

warn (WORN)—to tell about a danger that might happen in the future

All About Mysteries

A mystery is a story where the main characters must figure out a puzzle or solve a crime. Let's think about *The Mystery of the Fishy Canoe*.

Plot

In a mystery, the plot focuses on solving a problem. What is the problem in this story?

Clues

To solve a mystery, readers often look for clues. Did Pedro have any clues in this mystery? What tactics did he and his mom use to solve the mystery?

Red Herrings

Red herrings are bad clues. They do not help solve the mystery. Sometimes they even make the mystery harder to solve. Were there any red herrings in this story? Explain your answer.

Thinking About the Story

1. Katie and her mom were separated from Pedro and his mom for their canoe trip. Do you think it is a good idea to split up from your group when you are doing an outdoor activity? Why or why not?

2. What senses did Pedro and his mom use while retracing their steps? How did they use their senses?

3. Write your own outdoor adventure story. Be sure to include descriptions of things you might see in the nature setting.

4. Have you ever gotten lost or separated from other people? How did you feel while you were lost? How did you feel when you found your way again?

What's Inside?

To retrace their steps, Pedro and his mom used their senses. They smelled for the flowers and watched for the bird nest. Here is a fun activity where using your senses could reveal what's inside paper bags. You and your friends can take turns preparing mystery bags and guessing what's inside.

Mystery Bag Fun

What you need:

- brown paper bags

- a variety of items that can be examined using smell, touch, and hearing. Examples include lemon slices, flowers, pinecones, sugar, bells, and a bar of soap. Be creative and think of your own!

- a blindfold

What you do:

1. Put one object in each bag.

2. Blindfold a friend, then give them a bag to guess what's inside. They can smell, touch, or listen to the object. Once they have an idea of what's inside, they can take a guess.

3. Take turns gathering items and making mystery bags. You can even time each other to see who can guess correctly the fastest.

Solve more mysteries with Katie and Pedro!

KATIE WOO and PEDRO Mysteries

The Birthday Party Mystery

by Fran Manushkin • Illustrated by Tammie Lyon

KATIE WOO and PEDRO Mysteries

The Mystery of the Disappearing Treasure Map

by Fran Manushkin • Illustrated by Tammie Lyon

KATIE WOO and PEDRO Mysteries

The Mystery of the Fishy Canoe

by Fran Manushkin • Illustrated by Tammie Lyon

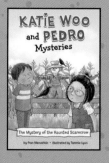

KATIE WOO and PEDRO Mysteries

The Mystery of the Haunted Scarecrow

by Fran Manushkin • Illustrated by Tammie Lyon

KATIE WOO and PEDRO Mysteries

The Mystery of the Missing Mummy

by Fran Manushkin • Illustrated by Tammie Lyon

KATIE WOO and PEDRO Mysteries

The Mystery of the Snow Puppy

by Fran Manushkin • Illustrated by Tammie Lyon

KATIE WOO and PEDRO Mysteries

The Mystery of the Stinky, Spooky Night

by Fran Manushkin • Illustrated by Tammie Lyon

KATIE WOO and PEDRO Mysteries

The Peanut Butter and Jelly Mystery

by Fran Manushkin • Illustrated by Tammie Lyon

KATIE WOO and PEDRO Mysteries

The Rainbow Mystery

by Fran Manushkin • Illustrated by Tammie Lyon

KATIE WOO and PEDRO Mysteries

The Super-Duper Supermoon Mystery

by Fran Manushkin • Illustrated by Tammie Lyon